SARDINE CAN

Jim Bell

www.jbellstories.com

to K & C

CONTENTS

INSANE VIA BADEN-BADEN

It was a pig of a crossing
as they lugged
their army packs
through the fuel yards;
collecting the dead
from the listing sloops
across the quay . . .

Scrawled across
the wide bloodied shore
were the trawlers' last words,
gouged deeply
into the soil,
by the dead hand
of every carcass,
in small, unintelligible mauls . . .

All their fingernails were red
with crusted earth
and blood;
but they were all illiterate,
and didn't know how to tell about
what had happened
in their scribbles
across the muck,
so they'd tried drawing diagrams
instead . . .

(Just their sheer attempt to
tore at everyone's hearts.)

A skinny parson
lay garrotted,
spreadeagled
in the middle of the town square,
with his entrails ripped out
by the baboons
— still belching near,
up high in the mpingo trees —
and he was still clutching tight
in a bony fist
that old black tome
in a mangy goose skin . . .

It was clear to the locals
that the *"spiritual gangsters"* of old
were on the march again.
All the corpses' faces

were cowered
into the cups of their hands
because of their initial fear of blushing.
It was their calling card;
their *"sign of adumbration."*

It was long rumoured
back in Timbuktu
that these *"outlaws of the soul"*
dwelt somewhere
in the deep lacunae of the Sahara,
where even the many traders
on their camels,
who knew the sands so well,
could never ascertain,
caravan after caravan . . .

Originally,
Private Morla first got wind
of this phenomena
years ago,
when, after having a sudden fit
in Baden-Baden
one summer
over his holidays,
he was committed to an asylum
in Herr Gaggle Street
for a time;
a sanctum where, inside,
all they ever did was research
"the science of defiance,"
and it was there

that he heard
the worst secrets
of the world . . .

His only cohorts there
was a local fig picker
and a firefighter,
who were both always
frothing at the jowls
in unison,
"Noon's the go,
noon's the go,"
like a couple of stir-crazed loons;
whilst all the others
reeled back in the shadows
and spilled
the beans on the world . . .

Each night
an orderly would strap Morla down
in an old hessian straitjacket
that was ironically handloomed
at a secret prison farm
in Quagadougou,
where his grandpa
long toiled for his sins
as a graverobber . . .

In a corner of the ward
sat a still, older woman called Giki,
with her blistered lips
forever pursed

to a rusty trombone,
softly playing
"Any Bone, Any Home,"
day and night,
dusk to dawn . . .

It was only because of Giki,
Morla learned
that he loved the voice
and clipped accent of the deaf,
and their relentless fetish
for music,
and the way
they'd dive at any rhythm,
just for the sheer, humane ambition
of getting everyone's blood dancing
at eight in the morning,
and good old eight
in the afternoon . . .

Late one night,
near the end of Morla's time there,
there was this old reminder of his youth
in Australia
that was suddenly fanned by
Giki's advances . . .

It was a baptism of fire
when he'd first come of age,
yearning for union all along;
but in the end,
he usually wound up

sulking off
somewhere
for the lack of luck
then apportioned him
in those days,
thinking
it was because
he was black . . .

"*Stop raining!*"
all the senior girls
would shout at him
from the bus windows
in passing . . .

Then,
at other times,
at sports carnivals,
when they'd all laughed
their mouths sore at him,
some of them
would crawl across the grass his way,
and dissolve him
in the crazy crank air;
with zydeco music in their ears,
and vindaloo fumes
under their noses,
as all the others
squelched around
in the distance
in their platypus soles . . .

He used to recite
homemade verses to them,
that he'd secretly whipped up
away from his kin,
like *"What Is Better,*
A God Without Teeth,
Or A God Without Eyes?"
or the long rhyming epic
many loved,
"I Am The Negro
Of The Ego."

The near Catholic college for girls
they all attended
was run by sad, old ex-nuns
of the war;
each with leashed schnauzers
forever heeled
at the hems
of their ballooning skirts . . .

They were all heady victims
of adoration,
recruited to become martyrs,
and deemed to long devour
gothic literature
as they obediently aged
into studied virgins,
fully trained
and devoted
to long condemning
the lofty ideals,

and romanticism,
of that ambiguous creed
they snarled
as *"Individualism"*. . .

Private Morla
and his squad
dourly buried the dead,
then moved on
to the next port
where it was all just as ruined
as everywhere else,
where no one cared for anyone
or for what they believed in,
or didn't,
anymore . . .

HACK'S BREAKFAST

The edges of her lover's eyes
are now black
from the burnt blood,
which she herself
had cauterized,
for recompense
of the lie
she had sought,
by any means,
to purge from her thoughts,
as a subterfuge
for what never was.

THE INSECT YEARS

The standard ploys resume.
It's a quick-fix world.
Sign language everywhere,
and aside,
the same old failing groans . . .

Old homeless Foley
— long bent by fluids —
with his garbled mind
forever stuck on sour,
only ever gleans
Johnny 3:16 as:
"A pox on both your balls and holes!"

Outside, under stars,
the streetwalkers
on Darling Street
softly proselytize

in the racket
to all those storming
the Easter sales:
"Shine on, savage sin!"

But with them alone,
late at night,
sharing tram shelters
from the rain,
they whisper behind hands,
like friends,
telling Foley the bigger toll:
*"You only desire something
in order to stop wanting it."*

When Foley turned up sober
at the soup chamber
Maundy Thursday,
he dropped a scrawled prayer
into the flak box
and said aloud to himself,
like all the others:
"I am a grieving multitude."

Later, he stood up on queue,
with two hands full
of dripping on bread,
and sang the join-in chorus sing-a-long
to the old street ode,
"The Shit-Glory Tree."
*"♫ Only the squeaky wheel
ever gets the oil . . . ♫"*

The concierge
lays out the facts
before them all;
so that they'll get along
for the dinner
and for the day . . .

How everyone eats . . .
How everyone excretes . . .
How everyone flatulates . . .
How everyone masturbates . . .
How everyone lies . . .
How everyone cries . . .
How everyone dies . . .

Foley soon fades out
after gorging,
like some of the others do,
not used to a full belly
since Christmas Day.
It's like when a cat wails out lonely,
it always naps him out . . .

He sleeps
like he feels that the dead
still hate him for all eternity;
as outside,
the wide shiny leaves
shed from the plane trees
like a thousand
wept Australias . . .

WILD DOG VALLEY

Ironically,
his given name is Wynn.
His apparent cross is *"World View"*.
He has a bent look
from a lazy eye now.
Once, as a boy,
he worshipped the Nazarene
fixed to a rood of larch
above a doorjamb,
before the state
severed his faith
from *"The worldwide sham"* . . .

It all began
on the muddied Burmese shores
of the river Irrawaddy,
when Wynn
was gently stamping butterflies
into the earth,
to sell to tourists
at all the stalls,
where they all haggled over
stacked rug mountains,
and whittled marmalade dolls,
and all the snub-nosed monkeys
packed away in crates
as pets . . .

He used to trade
dumdum bullets
for the eggs of dodos,
and cut-throat blades
for rotting peppers,
and homemade grenades
for canned nutmeats,
before the evil prospered again
and the *"pisskeepers?"* returned
to try to resolve everything
all over again . . .

Incessant melees
between the junta
and ethnic rebel groups
were breaking out
across the ranges
like the olden days,
and before long
a U. N. Protection Force
(UNPROFOR)
was engaged in fire . . .

Wynn was soon *"spotted,"*
and suddenly deemed
a field assistant
to a U.N. medical unit,
on account
of his unofficial *"dwarfism"*
— *"He'll get to the wounded good"*—
but was soon employed
to sneak into battle

to rub chrism
on the eyes of the dead;
so their souls
wouldn't be syphoned off to Hades
as the moon
began to wane . . .

Wynn had met many a footman
from another land,
who were all just barely alive,
and on their last breaths,
and he often caught
their strange final words
on the earth,
as he lay at their sides,
about the din,
to begin the anointing
of the oil . . .

One old soldier
softly said to him
between gasps:
"All the op shops . . .
are full of nothing . . .
but Division Four . . .
and Matlock threads."
Whatever that meant.

A younger gunner
giggled to him
in a dying fit:
"It's like a loaded dice . . .

Pubic hair
always lands as a six."

And another one
whispered to the sky:
"Is there anyone . . .
chiselling away in Paree?. . .
I want to begin again! . . .
Straight away!"

At night,
huddled in the trenches,
all the officers and surgeons
sipped at rich bean soup
from silver spoons,
and discussed
the philosophical pleasures
and displeasures
of certain body politics;
as the muddied rest of them,
out in foxholes,
shovelling spam,
listened to the braying flocks of ducks
fleeing low
across the night sky . . .

And then they all saw them,
flapping by for their lives,
lit by the light of exploding shells;
the whole sky burnt
with an orange sick.
Hung birds; slow emulsifiers . . .

There was a large wooden shed
set up along the banks
of the Irrawaddy,
where all serving forces
could gather
to let down their hair.
There were always a few
of the local starving girls there,
pawning off their bones
for the merest of coins,
just to feed their starving families
waiting in the glens.
All the *"pisskeepers"*
called them *"Marion,"*
or drunken derivatives of *"carrion,"*
because they all seemed
"So weird". . .

This establishment was called
"THE TWO MAGGOT CAFE".
It was a rickety box,
whipped up
from the scrounged debris
of the many bombed-out huts nearby,
and tied together
with used gauze
and antiseptic bandages . . .

Shell-shocked soldiers
would end up
sitting alone in filthy corners,

dreaming of their distant inamoratas,
and all that
they'd once meant to them;
their all-of-a-sudden
whitened hair
held in their trembling fists
like plucked weeds
from the world's
oldest graves . . .

AN OPEN CAGE

To Warwick
— prized heart surgeon
about town —
the valves become her eyes
as she blinks on
that old charm
when he sees a rhythm
kick in again . . .

Tucked inside the muscle
is her mind,
the vagaries of memory;
where flippant words of love
are ployed
like puppets
are played to lie . . .

He sees each chamber
as her mouth
— the back-biter,
the sniper,
the skite
and the lark —
swallowing down
every hallowed morsel
sent in muck;
but when it pounds,
it's her swearing to kill him
"in one swoop"

like she'd long swore
she would,
"one day" . . .

He wants it
to turn into a dove
— like her heart once was,
not so long ago —
but he's stuck now
with just the plain old her
in memory
she gave everyone else
at the end . . .

What would happen
if he spoke to a bird
and pretended
it was an earlier her?
Would it flee as well?

Though now,
every one of them
flitting around
screams at him the same.
He used to think
they were delicate things,
and then wondered
if it was him
all along . . .

But the whole of spring
has passed,
and against his chest
is not her dove anymore;
but just a parked, sloven owl
inside
too weary to budge
an inch . . .

THE CANNIBALS' MOOR

Acts of kindness
are not required anymore.
People are too scared
by their own
overwhelming spells
of gratitude now . . .

But poor old Annie Trope
of 19th Beach
dreams only
of her donkey ride to heaven;
knowing that,

with her flying pig tattoos
on her feet
— where once as a girl
she'd hoped the wounds of stigmata
would surface —
she could not ever drown
in the dark coming tide
of her own end . . .

Her days
simply waste away now,
as she sits alone
in her ragged gown,
by the stone hounds
towering high above the sea,
watching the shoals
of manta rays below,
hoovering the lagoons
of all plankton . . .

"Here," she whispers,
tapping at her bony chest,
looking down at the shallows
in a tease,
*"are more soft spots
to be prodded."*

She all so unemotionally
geometrizes
the increasing revelation
of her appearing skeleton,
as near her,

in the shade of a rusting elm,
the crumbling tombstone
of her old de facto,
"Detective" Boris
— her one and only Algonquin love,
lain name down
as a windbreak
to a maggie's egg —
slowly dwindles away
in the harsh salty winds,
with a hoon's wry graffiti,
"I'M IN LOVE WITH
HITCHCOCK'S DAUGHTER"
cut across its back
as it mosses . . .

She often sits there
at the cliff's edge,
on her makeshift bench,
and fondly recalls
all of his old tales of justice;
and how Boris
always openly winced
at the sheer Oedipal ugliness
of the coast's grinning priests . . .

"Their putrefied gums,
and their mummified flesh,
as they ramble on
with their Freudian slips
and gaffes."

And she'd think
of his infectious laugh,
and how it'd always take some time
to settle down
before firing up again;
and how he'd never sleep
when he was happy:
"A waste of joy is a blatant crime."

She can't believe the new adage
— *"Prosperity is guaranteed*
by science" —
being bandied about
by everyone now.
"Science never helped HIM,"
she'd always harrumph
to herself . . .

And how now
all the little birthday girls in town
are being given dolls with menses;
all of it an affront
to the sacred memories
of her own blessed 'hood . . .

Sometimes she recalls
how her only child, Deliska,
used to give her pet bat
a bath
on the weekends,
and how she'd always say:

"The best compliment
you can give someone,
is by saying
you think they're telepathic.
That's the goal of us all, mummy.
It's the most beautiful thing."

And how she often pined
to her untimely end
that all contact is only in tandem
with the vainglorious by-laws
ever granted
under *"stately progress"*:
1. Ego
2. Greed
3. Discourtesy.

~

Old Annie looked out
to the wharves
and watched everyone unload
the cargoes
of indigo dye again . . .

Along the wide shore,
the five blind artists of the shire
were dragging
the washed up jawbone of a whale
across the sand

— embroiled as usual
in the notion of closure —
arguing across the sea winds
over the old set laws
of the Gestalt Theory of Perception;
that by not completing the circle
as such,
they would never fully engage
with the same charms of reality
freely apportioned everyone . . .

She then recalled
the severity
of the *"sand plague"*
that orphaned her youth,
and how everyone in town
succumbed to the throes
of a certain insidious botulism
that swept the coast,
excepting her . . .

She remembered
how her parents
were in the parlour that night,
and how her mother
was seated at the ivories,
as her father
gurgled his sax to the moon,
and then how they both
— synchronistically —
had their first attacks;
and how her mother

suddenly vomited green
across the keys
as her father spurted up blood,
instead of saliva,
through the spitting valve,
and how they both
fell to the floor together
at a certain reverberating note
— and how the hell
all that hell
had followed her
all her days
ever since!

And how, now,
all she does is wile away
the lonely nights,
surfing channels in bored horror,
and in the sullen throes
of re-living
her own butchered montage
of patchy memories
and longings . . .

"Just one un-sorry step,"
she softly says to herself,
staring out across the sea
to the sky,
as the salty winds
burrow out the ends
of all her wrinkles . . .

Just one un-sorry step
to its spine,
and the lifting dawdle
of its humble travel
to her Lord . . .

Just one more
un-sorry step
to fall . . .

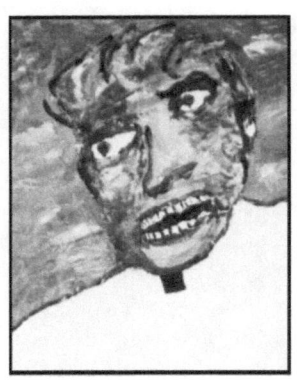

THE CROONER

In the orange tree town
of Fickidity Fickidity,
young Denny Angel
of Agama Grove
squirmed at his wooden desk
in class,
dressed in his brand-new
pristine school uniform.
Then he openly rebelled
against the old nun out front again,
who was deifying
yet another ancient butcher
of history
to be studied . . .

His initial attempts
were feeble though.
Just to help eclipse

any further slights of truth
from reaching the ears
of his friends,
he loudly voiced to someone
across the classroom
of his desire
to be a famed deep·sea diver,
just like his courageous
but imaginary dad,
Jacques Cousteau
— or *"J. C.,"*
as he'd say with a wink —
and everyone giggled at him
for how cheeky
he always was . . .

There were a set series
of lit neon signs
propped up
about the panes of class
that professed certain hallowed notions
for all to follow
on the way through life;
archaic rules of import
that have never been
wholly embraced
by a dozen faiths,
like kindness,
and forbearance,
and whimsies like that . . .

One sign
was for the shared motto,
"SILENCE IS GOLDEN"
and "OBEDIENCE
TEMPERS THE SOUL"
but it never lit up anymore.
(Denny had swiped every fuse
it was issued.)

Sometimes during lessons
he'd softly hum a tune to himself
when some dull fact
would be served up
to everyone again,
to be chewed on
for the millionth time by rote . . .

Lately, he'd dream of a song
he'd recently overheard
on a late night TV show
his foster-mum was glued to,
which the school
had long warned about
ever watching,
because of its dilapidated
standards of censorship . . .

Denny had once seen on this show
sepia footage of a native man
who'd just returned home
to his Stone Age village

after experiencing
at first-hand
modern life in a Western land . . .

But now, his old friends hated him,
because his family
had let their stock go to ruin
— disgracing themselves in the process —
and all he had left
were five small pigs,
and he felt ashamed . . .

All the sows of his pen
had been pawned off
for Shylock rates
while he was away,
ruining his chances
of ever advancing the tribe,
for which he'd sought
First World knowledge
to help them all
prosper together . . .

He'd learned
all sorts of strange things
in the New World,
like what *succubus*
and *satraps* were,
and what *codicils*
and *haecceity*
and *emoluments* meant . . .

He'd also developed
a tricky bed stress
in the chase
for lasting winks over there,
a thing he'd never known before
by the marshes,
where he was long soothed
in his hammock
by the twilight chattering
of the cassowaries
dallying nearby
in the brambles . . .

On his return home,
everyone in his village
was singing the ancient song of loss
for his grieving family
and their state of affairs:
the unforgivable bankruptcy
of their harbour of swine:

*"They are all short of days,
and if the night never ends,
all their souls
will soon be snatched away.*

*Like the time given flesh,
and all the blessed gifts
God had once bestowed
upon them all."*

~

After Sister Petronella
— aka *"Punchinella"* —
lectured the students
about an old ruling in France
on the banning of tunnels
for military purposes,
they then discussed
how selflessly St. Peter
was crucified upside-down
by choice
so as not to demean
the meaning further
of his Lord's sacrifice . . .

But Denny Angel
heretically voiced
the apposite view;
that no man taken to his cross
was ever given a last request,
and that he quite probably
had been nailed
the wrong way up
so as to intrinsically demean
his Lord's murder
in the eyes of the world . . .

Denny then asserted to class
that all these assemblies
and concoctions

of life's strange truths
and histories,
double-edged
as each often were,
often lured many
to the empathist's burrow,
embattled by
the still long heralded
"revolution by information"
in that ancient land and time.
And that was the first time
he ever mentioned the word
"propaganda,"
which pricked up
everyone's ears
in the back rows . . .

Often, Denny would ask the tutors
many alarming questions
never meant to be broached.
One day in class
he was severely maimed by a nun
when he brazenly asked
if the celibate heroes of history
had ever *"gotten off on their own,"*
putting forth the newly aired notion
that the act was *"entirely normal,"*
as he'd seen discussed
on the late show
he was forbidden
by the school
to ever watch at home . . .

Or, he suggested alternately,
that these giant historical figures
were all, in fact, eunuchs,
which the historians
for some reason
had chosen to *"redact"* . . .

But he was savagely lashed at
with a cane for that one,
whilst still seated at his desk.
And the nun chased him
all over the classroom
as she viciously struck at him,
again and again,
till finally she cornered him
near a dunce on its stool,
and flayed at him
in repetitive blows,
cutting through his shirt,
right down to his baby-fat
and his jangling nerves . . .

A similar thing happened to him
the year before
at a different parish.
For Show and Tell,
a boy once brought in
one of his dad's oldest toys
— a tin Batmobile —
and Denny openly joked
of how he wanted to ask Santa

for a Popemobile,
and how he saw in his mind
a Pope show on TV,
like the caped crusader's,
called *"Vatman,"*
and how a searchlight
would shine a crucifix in the sky
each Friday night,
and Vatman would slide down
a golden staff to his grotto,
in his giant hat,
and zoom off
in his tall glass car,
all to save someone
from eating a sausage . . .

And they took the strap
to him
for that one,
then and there,
right in front of all
the screaming girls;
about a dozen hot, gashing lashes
around his calves,
that would forever leave
a series of scars,
as if he'd been mauled
by a lion . . .

~

Over time,
as a brooding adolescent,
Denny was soon attending a school
not affiliated with faith
for the first time,
and where soon,
as puberty reared,
a certain lust welled within him
for a new pock-faced,
but statuesque young temp
in a flimsy skirt . . .

In his busted teenage eyes
full of longing,
Ms. Rhonda seemed to smoulder
the densest forests
of question marks into the sky,
with her swirling scents
wafting by him every day,
soon drugging him
into a lovesick delirium;
and he'd suddenly feel like the day
was just the playground
of their hearts,
as if the universe
was just theirs alone,
and that he alone was hers
and the world's only hero . . .

He used to ask her
loaded questions at lunchtimes,
to try to make her laugh,

after his peers
had bolted out the back
to play lacrosse . . .

"Miss Rhonda?
If the island of Crete
changed its name,
like Burma did,
would that make all its citizens
ex-Cretians?"

But she'd just let them wash by her.
Though, one day,
he once said to her
as an aside,
but in all seriousness,
spurred on by the recent antics
of a drunken neighbour
the night before:
"Only people with dentures
dislike long words
and rich vocabularies."

And she grew to smile at him.
He was a jaded 16,
and she was a splintered 21.
And she soon seduced him
by the blackboard one lunchtime,
and he left school,
a year on,
somewhat more than altered . . .

He soon formed a rock band
called Poverty Line.
He wore a ruby-red bombin
riddled with bullet holes,
and a white suit
with a reversed vicar's collar,
and sang rebellious songs
about his torturous life
as a beggar on a golden stool.
But, after years of slogging it out
in the traps,
little by little,
his muse wearied,
and he lost his passion . . .

In time,
he did fewer shows about town,
and soon became eco-aware,
and all of a sudden
turned strangely respectable,
and started to openly campaign
for the extermination
of all rodents
across the biosphere;
all for the secret sake
of replenishing
his dying step-pop's
pepper crops up north,
which he'd long hoped to inherit
for his pension
— save the rabbits.

And then,
in his midlife years,
after trouncing decades
of unnotable stages,
mouthing the same old tunes,
he finally gave it away,
and returned to school at night;
then six years later
branched out
as Chief Counsel
in Entertainment Law,
and was soon representing
many of his old ruined peers,
of the thousand dressing-rooms
of their youth . . .

And his fees
were explicitly obscene
in lieu of his total loss of love,
and the dour, changeless life
he seemed to endure.
But, however the old songs
of his peers
seemed to provoke in him
nostalgic reveries
of the many glorious times
he'd once reaped
as a minor star,
when he was all so young
and in love with life,
he died an heirless bachelor
in a wrecking yard,

haggling over a door-handle
for his rusty Citron;
forever unfulfilled
for never making
a comeback . . .

FIREBALL

She's like a caterpillar
tramping on the inside,
gorging all the foliage within;
or a worm in his heart
swallowing down everything
he's ever felt
in his life . . .

Nearly six months have passed
since they locked eyes.
No, it was dark
when they last spoke,
and it wasn't eyes,
but horns . . .

On the last, long drive home,
elbow out as usual,
head in his hand,
tears rolled like a spilled fuel
all the way down his arm,
and ran loose
along the rusted body
of his car
at high speed,
dribbling down the earth-strap
trailing the road,
and all that was left behind of her
were sparks
— the whites of the eyes
of the drivers

in back
lit up like ghouls
in a horror film.

THE CITRUS GIRLZ

On the wingtip of every bird
bleeds the pressing fingerprint
of man,
and in the ornery town
of New Roglia,
under the eerie
Do Nothing Trees
— out far by all the swirling ponds —
lay all the local *"court whores"*
at ease,
spieling colourfully
of their contempt
for all men's woes . . .

"My great-grandpa
had a wooden plate in his skull,"
one called Myra,
wheezed with relish
as she toked,
"and twigs and buds
grew out of his nose every spring,
and when he spat up
in his trusty cup,
all he ever exhumed
were splinters,
shavings and petals."

"I just softly burped,"
her ex·cellmate, Lucy, countered,

"and there was the raw taste
of sulphur on my palate,"
and she drained
the dregs of a wine cask
down her throat . . .

The 12 of them were coined
"The Citrus Girlz"
by the jittery populace of the town,
who were quite in awe of them all;
not just because
of the sheer blatant pride
they each displayed
for their own ends,
or for the disarming way
they'd all just freely let loose
their tricky laughs
when lounging along the banks
of The Thousand Icy Ponds,
eating fallen cumquats
and clementines,
with their stout, red dogs
lazing tame on the weeds
like a small flock
of newly devilled lambs
— but because they knew
of all their old crimes,
done over the years in town,
and the paltry time
they'd each done inside,
"just for kicks"
all along . . .

As a motley gang
they'd often wander about,
in a spaced-out haze,
around the rims
of the many swirling waters;
plucking meat flowers
from the marshes,
and lifting their tops
to the Kings of The Road
roaring by in their rigs,
like old sirens
besotted with the glimpse
of fleeting warriors . . .

In a little clearing ahead
between ponds
were the local foot-and-mouth painters,
holding brushes
between toes and teeth,
as they traced the view
unfolding before them all.
But when they saw
The Citrus Girlz approach,
they packed up their paintboxes fast,
and folded up their pics
with their brushes like beaks,
and zoomed back
along the gullies
in their chairs,
in search
of more tranquil zones . . .

At the end of one jetty,
stuck out like a knife
into a singularly freezing,
swirling chaos,
researchers
of the Chocolate 5th Laboratories
were filming
the shifts of yabbies
ambling in the shallows,
but could soon be heard
muttering *"Monstrance!"*
on seeing the Girlz approach,
and were fleeing back
to their trikes,
and puttering off
in the hunt
for more remote lagoons . . .

On the reddest stretch
of earth ahead,
a sweating man in a vest
— flanked by a dozen pups,
jointly leashed
to the ghostliest gum in sight —
was quickly bicycling
on his back,
all for the sake
of his precious hams:
a jogger on the lam,
with the deep vain fetish
for his own
flowering musculature.

But he didn't see
The Citrus Girlz approach.
And they all quietly
crept up on him,
and surrounded him,
and looked down
at his clenched eyes,
as his tree-trunk legs
peddled the empty sky,
and coquettishly asked him
as a choir:
"Are we there yet?"

Later that Saturday night
all the locals
flocking to the pub in town
for the "dinner special"
were soon tossing stones
at the same old, fat drunken wino
snoring across the steps
of the church
on the corner again . . .

But then,
come closing time,
when they were all shoved outside
to go home again,
they were soon
grovelling drunk to him
for help
on seeing the gang arrive . . .

The Citrus Girlz
were clearly waiting for them all
in the shadows;
all of them drugged up and rowdy,
and on the shakedown for cash
to get more,
with all their starving dogs
squealing
and straining on leashes
to run them down . . .

But the locals
kept on trying to wake the wino up,
with no success
— bloodied stones
all around his face —
begging him
for their lives
and their exoneration . . .

CLAPPERCLAW

He washed his eyes
when he was blind,
but now they've closed
and he dusts them . . .

Inside his mind
there lies a lie;
the inference of a word
called *"injustice"* . . .

He fed his hogs
the apple brains;
his dogs,
the cat's last muster . . .

The crow's first calling card
has cried,
and now his heart
is busted . . .

"We've got no smiles,"
the radio plays,
*"and ne'er a clue
on how to."*

HELL AND HIGH WATER

They both grew up
in the country town
of Seven Gills.
It was a mindfucked hellhole!;
the whole place
gaping for air
like a dying sole . . .

Young Dial,
a salad-faced man
with sickle-cell anaemia,
was playing cards
in the Boom Boom Room
of the Rutunta Hotel
on the Gold Coast.
Sitting beside him
was his chirpy, alopecian pal

called Figaro,
who looked like Richard Widmark
in an eye-patch,
laughing . . .

They were both on a quest
to finally free themselves
from the private school posturing
they'd each developed
over the years
at a ritzy boarding school
in the bush . . .

For a time at the hotel
they shared a disconsolate girl
from the west
called Juanita.
She was addicted to
rock 'n' roll glamour,
and obsessed with the mind-set
of all budding
assassination theorists . . .

Ubiquitous by nature,
psychotropic by constitution,
she worked as a picker too,
on a baron's
nearby cherry orchid,
where they all met,
working up the east coast
on their gap year . . .

One day,
out fishing on Gonquo Heel Pier,
Dial wisecracked to her
about how Bach
had fathered 20 kids,
and how he was chiefly
a church musician
who had addled his mind
*"from playing with his organ
all day long,"*
and Juanita
laughed herself silly,
as she tipped backwards
off the edge,
holding onto her knees,
and she somersaulted down
into the choppy sea
and was never seen again . . .

Days on,
re-emerging to the light,
and looking for something more
to snort,
Figaro soon stepped into the room
that was backwards;
for he was quite partial
to the ventriloquist's art,
and he always ended up
having more socks
on his hands
than his soles
ever wheeled . . .

Later, after lunch,
he was outside on the landing
with everyone else,
sitting purblind
and barely rested,
saluting a relentless fly
as he yawned,
awaiting the passing
of the inchoative waitress
he once mythically thought of
as Dymphna.
But he didn't feel armed
with his usual confidence,
and planned to chat with her
another time
when he felt less hungover
and splintered.
So he drank
more hair of the dog,
feeling even more miserable . . .

He felt just as gutted
about Juanita
as Dial did,
who was still inconsolably hammered,
and holed up in their hotel room.
But for some reason,
Figaro suddenly felt more than torn
about all of his family's
old foibles again . . .

Figaro's pop
was the local doctor in town,
who'd revealed to his son,
in his many drunken ramblings
over the years,
the identities of several patients
he'd diagnosed
with terminal maladies
— but he could never tell
any one of them.

Soon back home,
once Figaro found out
who was who,
he'd track each patient down,
and study their form
for a while,
then gradually ingratiate himself
into their lives,
and spend the rest of their days
cheering them on,
just to make them feel
more comfortable
before it was all over,
because his pop
never found the courage
to confront them all,
and Figaro always felt
he had to compensate
for the lack of will
his pop unduly suffered . . .

RONDO

To the public eye,
Rondo commands a chilly air.
Gargantuan in size,
he looks unruly,
and untamed,
with the tattooed scroll
of screaming mandrakes
around his throat;
and the hair's all wild,
and he's always got
this five o'clock shadow on,
like one of the old Beagles
in a favourite *"duck rag"*
he used to love as a kid.
And he wears dark clothes
all the time,
and he's always blinged out
in studs and skulls;
and he's gruff with everyone,
and never says a word
to a soul . . .

He recently performed surgery
on himself
to perfect the scare.
With a scalpel
swiped from a pawn shop
— along with an antique
dental syringe kit —

he drunkenly tried to sever
the 17 muscles responsible
for scaffolding a smile,
and wound up
cutting off his tongue
and nearly circumcising his head
into the bargain . . .

You could tickle him
like a baby now,
tell him the world's most deadly joke,
and his mouth
wouldn't budge a twitch.
But it's all just a front anyway.
He's heavily into romance . . .

Sometimes he shops incognito
at a distant mall
to rent out ancient movies,
like *The Goodbye Girl,*
and *Barefoot In The Park,*
and *Summer of '42,*
and *Marty* . . .

He watches them all,
week by week,
binging alone at home
on candy and cola
and tissues
like a teenage girl,
looping the most moving scenes,

over & over,
catching the subtlest nuance,
a look,
a smile,
a near tear,
a sigh,
again & again,
weeping himself silly
from all the hope
that reels him in
every time . . .

It's the sudden promise of harmony.
He's sucked in,
hooked bad
to the happy end,
and he can't get out.
He's got some sort of skewed notion
about love.
It's an old-fashioned
Hollywood kind
that gleams like a jewel,
and there's no evil left
anywhere
anymore . . .

But after he returns them
to the store,
he chucks the whole deal
back to hell again,
and stalks back out
amongst the crowd;

and everyone side-steps him
to one side,
as always,
wherever he goes,
like he's a bikie,
or an ex-con,
because he looks like
he's going to kill someone
before they kill him,
because he can't love anyone
before they love him . . .

BOX SAVIOUR AND
THE CREMATION KING

Local legend,
Skim Dreck
— of a once regional fame
in country athletics —
had chosen his newborn son's name
as Martin;
but at the hospital,
a dyslexic midwife
scribbled down *"Martian"*
on the tiny band
around his son's wrist,
and ever since then,
his first day on earth,
Martin was treated oddly in town
by everyone . . .

Though chiefly,
because his well-known
promiscuous mother
— Verena —
had died during childbirth;
and Skim was never regarded
as Martin's true father
from the start anyway . . .

All the locals
suspected Martin's real dad
was the just incarcerated madman

of the shire,
Verena's old school beau
— Corey Barclay Badar —
who'd just slit
the cudding throats
of all the town's heifers
over Lent
during a heatwave,
and was currently holed up
in the local clink
at Her Majesty's pleasure . . .

Father and son
lived in the sombre town
of God's Thumb,
where the giant sky
was always full of budgies
darting by,
with rainbows spouting everywhere,
as all the drunken tourists
straggled along the Jeeley River
to watch the napping black swans
drifting by
in the eerie shade
of the willows . . .

Skim Dreck drove
the town's only ambulance,
often currying moderate favours
for the many pensioned locals
suffering insomnia
across the valley,

long blamed
on the *"phantom thrum"*
of the nearby wind farm . . .

Duly, in an election year
— as a healing measure
the region over —
the state government
soon issued to all those affected,
therapeutical recordings
of ambient prenatal music
to relax to, and Skim
— always community-minded,
to help keep alive
the esteemed memory
of his own father's philanthropy
about town —
was now deemed
the good Samaritan gofer
for all those awaiting
the latest discography . . .

He'd often take
his toddler Martin along,
to show by example
the Christian pleasure
of helping others
less fortunate than themselves,
and together
they'd hand out the tunes.
It was Skim's *"Antidote to the blues"*. . .

But as the years rolled on,
Martin grew increasingly rebellious
to his father's churchy ways;
partly spurred on by his peers,
just to help sublimate
the sheer boredom
of the township . . .

Though, in the end,
Martin couldn't win
in any way with his dad.
His father's religious work ethic
had been drilled into him so well,
it soon affected his status
amongst his classmates,
who could barely comprehend
the overt piety
of his father's saintly deportment
about town . . .

Martin was too well spoken
for a start,
and seemed to be ruled
by a more than over-riding
sensitivity of conscience,
like the way he collected
all the old grey stones
from the train tracks,
and scribbled
"Auld Lang Syne!"
on every one,
to devotedly stack around

his mother's grave
each New Year's Eve;
whilst his peers
were always out
egging the old locals
as they wheeled
their shopping home . . .

Martin would try to fit in
with them all though,
and talk tough as them
at times,
but he could never
adopt it all in full . . .

He'd try to crack a joke
in a like vein,
but it would always
trip him up . . .

Instead of saying
— like them —
"Only taking the piss,"
he'd softly mumble,
as he blushed with a frown,
"Just fetchin' some urine there . . ."

So they started calling him
"The Sewer Prince,"
which soon evolved into
"The Cremation King,"
when he accidentally burned

a neighbour's cat to a crisp,
then two days later
the school's mascot quoll . . .

In his later,
much soured teenage years,
Martin met a girl called Marama
when he worked
as a part-time tarmac cleaner
at the nearby Red Bird aerodrome.
She worked
at the little wire ticket-gate
out front,
collecting flight passes,
and welcoming tourists
to the hallowed ground
of God's only thumbprint . . .

But it never washed
with his gang.
When he suddenly went to work there
—just to earn some cash
to drink away the time in town—
they all taunted him,
saying he'd just joined
"Ben Dover Inc."
Then when he met
the loving Marama,
they all changed tack,
and started teasing him
as a boy
"forever cunny struck". . .

Though all that
suddenly crashed with her,
when one night
she betrayed him
with one of the gang,
and Martin suddenly left the airfield,
and his father,
and the mess
that was God's Thumb,
and promptly joined the navy,
and was soon leaving
for peacekeeping duties
aboard the HMAS *Manangatang*,
where all he did,
bouncing across the waves,
was polish
the long grey decks
and gunnery . . .

~

Amongst the burly crew,
Martin didn't fare all that well.
A small select band of psycho sailors
coined themselves
"The Kidnap Commandos,"
and a pet prank
played on fresh recruits
was to lock them down
in a gun box
during drills

as they shelled dummy ships
for target practice,
just to keep themselves
buoyant between ports . . .

Though
there was a mess cook aboard
called Wirt who had a
"mild, integrative pleasure defect,"
and he'd often try to rescue
all those holed up like that,
just for fun . . .

Wirt was also the M.C.
for many of the shows
they put on below deck
to entertain themselves,
when they campily dressed up
as pin-ups and stars,
and acted out
blunt immorality plays
of the high seas.
And though everyone admired
Wirt's witty repartee on stage,
offstage, he was plain disliked,
though somewhat afeard
because of his physique . . .

But fearless
to the mob's inherent rebuff,
Wirt was always out
rescuing rookies

from all over the vessel.
He'd dragged up a dozen men
tossed over the side
in life-buoys
as a tease to sharks,
after being dragged for miles
by just a simple braid.
He'd untied others
who'd been hazed with kites,
and bound to cannons
and depth charges overnight.
He'd even doused out
a closet Buddhist on deck, who
— unable to take
any further ribbing
from the crew —
lit himself as a pyre,
vowing to return as a storm
to rock the sea
and swallow them whole . . .

Soon, because of Wirt's penchant
for rescue
at gun boxes,
he was soon christened
by all those on deck
as the *"Box Saviour."*
But it was only when
the *Manangatang*
collided with a sub one night,
and both ships began to sink
in the middle of the Pacific,

that *"Box Saviour"*
and *"The Cremation King"*
appeared within orbit
of each other . . .

Wirt and Martin
had each secured blow·up rafts
in the panic,
and were hauling aboard
the few enlisted survivors,
and were soon
each captaining their charges,
as they drifted aimlessly
with the tides.
But, as the days passed,
both men were soon forced to rule
on which failing crewmates
to cannibalise
for the sake of the many . . .

The most struggling recruits
on each raft
were soon picked off,
and duly dried out in the sun
as jerky,
and shared amongst both crews
— only restricting themselves
to *"the legs and wings"*.

Though sometimes,
on one raft,
one man would suddenly expire,

just after someone else
was sacrificed;
whilst at the same time,
on the other raft,
no one would die at all.
And on that raft
with the two dead,
most of the crew
would be more than full
from the first cadaver;
whilst all those starving
on the other raft had nothing.
So the raft with too much fare
would often pass over
the leftovers . . .

But, after all the carnage
that spilt into the sea
between them,
one raft suddenly burst
under the pinch of a dorsal fin,
and those few surviving
tried to scramble over,
till only one passed through
a frenzy of sharks
and climbed aboard
the last raft . . .

Box Saviour
and The Cremation King
were now together,
but neither of them could decide

on consuming the last man
for themselves,
because he seemed just as alert
and desperate to live as them . . .

Then the sailor
was elbowing at Martin,
that they both take Wirt out,
because he was so portly.
But Wirt clocked him with the oar,
and he and Martin
promptly took his wings . . .

And as the days passed on
through the storms,
still, there was no sight of land
or salvage.
Box Saviour
and The Cremation King
just sat at each end of the raft,
drifting idly along
for an eternity,
as the porpoises gently rose
to mock the rubber,
and each man
waited for the other
to tire,
so as to finally gorge
the last available morsel . . .

HER GHOST

When it's late in the night,
in the dying hours before dawn,
and he staggers back
to his room once more
— sitting on the side of the bed,
disrobing —
he often wonders
how he will think of her
this time,
when he turns out the light,
to lay down
on his stomach
and gag again.

Because he knows
he will think of her:
but how *this* time?
Lying on her stomach,
in her own bed
— alone again —
as she dreams of him,
drunk as well?

He gently trails his fingers
across the other pillow,
to feel the suppleness
of her skin,
then touches the mole
on his face,
thinking it hers
— how she had
the exact same button,
in the exact same spot —
and he pushes it,
like it's an intercom,
hoping she'll feel his touch
transposed
across the hilly miles,
as an old tenderness calling,
still freshly primed
to be sated . . .

VALE PERLITA

Lonely old money bags,
Vale Perang,
a former Olympic diving champ
— *"part newt,"*
some say in town —
lives as an eccentric recluse,
in a four storey building
lined with bomb-proof windows,
and with a pool on the roof
three floors deep,
and he often dives down to the street
to catch glimpses
of all the local sharks outside,
flitting along their own sea . . .

Years ago,
in his hey-day,
Vale once bought a sapphire ring
for a girl called Perlita,
but she shrieked back at him,
"Symbols?"
then spat at his chest,
and stormed off . . .

That night he dreamed
he coughed up blood
the next morning,
with a hole burned
right through his heart.

Missal spiders
were scuttling through his chest,
tying him to the side of the bed
with their webs.
He had to slowly gnaw his way out,
once they returned
to their nests
in the corners of the room.
Then he woke up,
and sought treatment
for his psoriasis
at the dispensary
where Perlita used to work,
and they first met . . .

Over time,
through the course
of his treatment,
Vale learned many things
of her recent past
from the old pharmacist
who knew Perlita well:
namely that she was once
the concubine
of a disbarred lawyer,
an unlicensed doctor,
and a defrocked priest . . .

"She had a penchant for men
obsessed with justice,
mercy, and faith,"
the pharmacist said.

He soon confided more to Vale;
that she had, in fact,
a mild criminal record,
a common terminal illness,
and an all-consuming
spiritual crisis of the soul . . .

For a time,
Perlita had lived the married life
of a good Christian wife
out in the suburbs,
before suddenly discovering
her breasts were riddled with worms
after attending communion
one cold Sunday dawn . . .

The initial misdiagnosis
by the local *"quack"* in town,
led to the discovery
that said *"sacred hosts"*
delivered to the parish that month
had been contaminated
in manufacture
by a deadly parasite
that had infiltrated the flour,
infesting the
— as yet, untransubstantiated —
"flesh of the Saviour,"
which soon wiped out
many of the local *"flocks"*
floundering in the backblocks
by the bay . . .

Then all of Perlita's doubts
about everything else
suddenly surfaced,
and she chose to redeem herself
through the knowledge
bestowed upon those few
endorsed with the power
to help relieve others
of their ills;
however foolhardy she felt
such efforts
would ever absolve a thing
in the end . . .

But the innate betrayal
of those old, raw forces
from within,
in lieu of her childlike bent
for unconditional trust,
would never relinquish
her desire
to be further enlightened
to the many mysteries
of law,
medicine,
and philosophy
— the three disciplines
that intimidated her
most.

THE PILLOW IS A SILENT SIBYL

Carlo's chronic insomnia
had left him crestfallen for years.
He'd long given up
on ever filtering his days
through the normal,
nocturnal activity of dreams,
and could only
— in vague efforts between naps —
allow his imagination
to freely roam
over the course
of an afternoon . . .

But, over time,
a subtle destabilisation
of his senses followed,
till one day
his doctor confirmed to him

that he'd long passed
the chance of ever
fully recovering
and reclaiming the night . . .

"In fact," he said to him,
"at this rate,
you're rushing head-on
into the arms of death."

Ticking off the symptoms,
Dr. Quatta queried Carlo further
of the imminent five stages
that might prelude his end . . .

1.   Did he have over-sleepiness
      during the day?

"Of course," he'd always had that.

2.   Did he feel lethargic at times?

"All the time," he said.
"It's like being held down
by some gigantic thumb."

3.   Did he ever suffer from otundation?

"Wha . . ?" he yawned back.

        "Do you sometimes maintain
        the inability to be woken?"

"Always," Carlo said.
"A bomb couldn't rise me at noon."

4.   Did he often feel in the throes
        of a rising stupor?

"That's a given," he mumbled.

Dr. Quatta diagnosed Carlo
had indeed passed
the first four
of the five procedural stages
before death,
and that it would only be
a matter of time
before his young patient
would breach
the final stage
and slide headlong
into a coma;
which soon happened . . .

Carlo had fallen
into a colossal daze
for weeks on end,
lumbering about town
like a zombie,
more moribund than usual,
before suddenly
he collapsed in the street
and was interred . . .

~

Under law,
Carlo Warwick Tambet
was laid in state in a coma
for over 30 years,
and compassionately attended to
by the A.E.C.C.
(Anti-Euthanasia Coma Committee)
— a legislated body,
established by several merging
conservative forces —
before suddenly waking
one summer noon,
in his mid-life years,
as a nurse finished lancing
his sores
with a scream . . .

But again, in time,
he soon felt inert
to the efforts of the world;
little knowing
how everything
had subtly altered
in his sleep . . .

Carlo soon learned that,
after a spell of quakes
that shook the globe
for a generation
as he slept,

the Leaning Tower of Pisa
had finally kissed the earth;
and that the floor
of the Grand Canyon
had been pushed up
till its void was filled;
and that the Pyramids of Giza
had collapsed
like houses of cards;
and the giant Jesus of Rio
had jumped into the lake;
and that all the other
Wonders of the World
now seemed
somewhat lessened . . .

And though initially,
over the first few days,
Carlo felt clearly robbed of time
— by time —
he soon began to embrace the notion
of all this sudden
levelling of everything,
like the way everyone else
around the world
seemed to be feeling about it
as well . . .

And the epiphany
of such a metamorphosis
of the world
— with lesser hype —

gave Carlo greater solace
to, in turn,
tease change in himself,
more broadly
than ever mused before
in his first spell . . .

So he resumed
his mistook span,
and finally took a chance on life,
traveling widely;
and soon wound up
in foreign digs,
wedding the last heir
to the Franking Machine,
and fathering
further trustees
into the fold . . .

MISTIME IN KUNNARD
Pop: ~~909~~ 905

His face swelling
with tiny lumps,
he wriggles loose the weights
from his spine
and wanders down the highway,
swatting the last bug
shooed out of town
— the caterwauling
still ringing in his ears —
his car just torched
on the corner . . .

*"We don't take to your kind
around here,"*
the publican snarled at him.
*"All you black-sheep-type-people
on the fringe."*

Local boozehounds
taped two bags of crushed ice
to his back
and sent him on his way;
everyone from the bar
pelting him with beer nuts
from the verandas
as he slowly passed by,
hunched over like an old man,
all of them laughing . . .

Come dusk,
old desert ghosts
straggled past him
on the other side of the road
as he hitchhiked
back home
— all of them hangdog —
but no cars came his way.

All the creatures of the night
soon started
on their crawlings,
to cross from one lot
to another,
but they would not receive him.
Attacked left, right, and centre,
he stamped them all dead,
all the way home . . .

But home was gone
in the end
— a cindered skeletal corpse
was all that was left
amongst the ashes.
Holding his wife's charred skull
in one hand,
a burnt bicycle chain
in the other,
he stormed back to town
to even up the score . . .

Those two bags of burning ice
were now his eyes.
His mouth,
the wick of a bomb . . .

HEART ON THE LINE
(Train to Melb.)

It's blue underneath,
from all the drained blood,
but its tips are white
when she holds on;
a willowy hand
held back behind her hair,
as if holding on her head
as well . . .

All the nails
are a blotched, fading black,
and a little bit chewed,
but there's no ring,
and the whole thing's raw . . .

From behind,
it makes Liam want to touch it
with a cheek;
feel the smooth suppleness,
like a puppy's coat
under his palm,
something pure and graceful . . .

Then she tucks it in again,
like she hears
all his cravings in back,
senses all the old longing

behind her,
and it disappears back under,
clasped by her lover's hand
again . . .

And Liam turns back to the glass
in the sunshine,
and bites his tongue
in the reflection of the pane,
with the blurring trees
and acres
being smeared
before him again,
in one long, single maul . . .

THE SHREDS OF MORLAND

In a musty hospice bed
old Morland cuds over
the ancient social codes
of his youth
for the millionth time,
and the same backsliding
recidivism
he always succumbed to
along the way,
chewing over and over
the old sense
— and absence —
of each memory
still inhibiting him . . .

At the wire-meshed pane,
the old sodic moon
hangs in the sky
like a savoured medal,
and all Morland does
is stare ahead in a trance,
like an elephant in a zoo
with ghosts in its eyes,
keening nothing
that is ever forgiven
or forgotten . . .

He will remember,
as long as memory is,
the sigh of a lone viola . . .

One night,
it issued from a nearby loft
to his hideout,
when he was a shell-shocked deserter
on the run in Switzerland
during WW1,
and he often crooked an ear
to hear it more clearly,
as he eavesdropped
on the composer
to more calmly recuperate;
for it soothed him . . .

Then he'd hear Igor
vent his spleen
about Strauss again;

*"Whichever purgatory
punishes
triumphant banality!"*[1]

Morland once heard him
laughing
with a friend
about a starving vegan sculptor
they both knew
whose chickens
only ever died of old age,
and they both cackled till dawn
like madmen . . .

Often though,
on those frozen winter eves,
music would never
be played.
But still,
out on the landing,
Igor's wildest notions,
openly voiced to his muse,
in intemperance
and heady frustration,
would make Morland's head swim,
as did always
his welcome intonations . . .

---

[1] *Conversations With Igor Stravinsky* by Igor
Stravinsky and Robert Craft P. 75

"All music will be mood-classified!"[2]
Igor declared
across the dozing world:
"Kaleidoscopic montages
for contortuplicate personalities!
Simultaneous concerts
binaurally disaligned
to soothe both men
in the schizophrenic!"[3]

In his dank single bed,
Morland recalled how then,
in those early days
of his freedom
from the war,
the only dreams
he ever truly weaved
or whetted . . .

But old Igor is dead,
and his viola
sighs nevermore.
Except on the radio,
as Morland lies waiting . . .

---

2 Ibid. P. 131
3 Ibid. P. 131

HIT AND MYTH

Pershing was Northern Territory bred.
Progeny of Maroochy,
the Creatrix.
Nursling of Ariel,
the Protectress.
Now a cuckold of XXXX,
the Destructress . . .

As a boy,
he would often slip away
to lay still
in the tall spinifex grasses
across the ranges,
so as to freely dream away the hours,
finally free
from all the others
always blundering about him,
retching,
and laughing,
all emaciated as mantises,
and all their ratty dogs
with bleeding money-pockets
under his toes . . .

The vastness
of the massive sprawl
of his backyard alone
had long served
as a psychic exchange
for everyone in the bush,

and a lot
long self-replenished
as the only known church
there ever was . . .

They used to shout out to him:
"You dreaming again, Persh?"
And he'd bark back, proudly:
"Me being my myth."

And he'd shuffle off,
free from the township
and the roads,
back out to all the trees
and anthills again,
with a million leaves
crunching under his soles . . .

"You be myth?"
they'd keep shouting after him,
drunk and laughing.
"I be myth,"
he'd mumble back
over his shoulder.

Pershing had these secret mental wings
that always lifted him
above the fray.
Whereas, everyone else
only had their little chicken switches
to gamble with;

Wasn't Lizzie the only one
who made her feel better
all the time?
Because she felt dead inside
— she thought to herself —
and Lizzie didn't.
She then realized
Lizzie was the bliss all along,
and not her . . .

She was working all this out
in the backyard one night,
when her parents
were fighting inside
as usual . . .

Then her father
poked his head out the door
in sudden light,
and screamed at her:
"Get rid of that thing!
Don't bring it inside again!
There's crap everywhere!"

After the door slammed
and the darkness returned,
Jishy was in a rage,
staring up at the full moon;
and she slowly got to her feet,
and with all her might
suddenly tossed Lizzie
its way

— disappearing over the roof next door —
so that she'd live,
and that the source of her bliss
was dead,
and she'd finally grow up . . .

~

Twenty years on . . .
Jishy's all grown up now.
She's got a fully formed adult face,
and stretch-marked breasts,
and child-bearing hips
from faring twins,
and a tall well-to-do husband,
and a big windowed house
filled with shoes
and frocks,
and she eats
of the finest foods
and wines . . .

But really, in the end,
it was just all too perfect.
She realised
there was just too much bliss,
and that it all had to be stopped,
so that she'd grow up
— even though
she was now fully grown.

It was very difficult for her.
Her parents were dead,
but their voices
long rang in her ears.
And her teachers were gone,
and all her old friends
on the other side of town.
There was only the TV left,
she realised,
to pass the old message on,
on how to kill bliss
more lastingly . . .

And so she finally did it.
Destroyed it all at once.
Her precious home and family.
All her security and comfort.
Then she was locked away
in the confines of a cell,
and all the bliss was gone,
and suddenly
she felt all grown up . . .

Except now,
everyone wanted to kill her.
But she couldn't understand why,
because she'd killed
all the bliss,
and was now
all grown up . . .

And then she realised,
they hadn't grown up,
and were only set to
end her
in the same flippant way
she'd blindly sacrificed
her *"Dear Elizabeth,"*
so that the source
of their bliss
was dead,
and that they'd all grow up . . .

SUFFERERS' PARADISE

The young and astute artist,
Ballyhoo Halfahorse,
was delicately painting
in gouache,
"Still Life With A Mouse,"
as he listened
to the midday news
on community radio:
". . . All the old councillors,
who long boasted
of their incorruptibility record
in The City of Churches,
clandestinely helped
lead the mounting hysteria
in the streets,
much like the way
hyenas always lead
the jungle din."

Whilst out on the landing,
overlooking the Pacific,
his green-eyed, sultry lover,
Candy Trax,
sat glued to the exploits
of Acquila and Darrow
in a turgid, pisstake TV soap,
"As The Gusset Runs . . ."

Darrow was an autopsist
in the terrorist's *"Funderground"*.
He was taping
a corpse's genitalia to its leg,
to keep it out of harm's way
during the exploratory,
when the phone rang,
which he picked up
with a bloodied glove:
the receiver was stained
all purple by now,
from the spilled icy juices
of the many cadavers
he'd opened up
over the years
and examined.

"Mister Bleh-said,
that is just sheer baby talk.
I have no time
for your further discreditations
at this juncture,"
and he hung up,
and returned
to the rectal examination
of the shanghaied mayor . . .

Candy groaned out loud
as another ad suddenly came on
about Rice Bubbles,
and everyone was happy
and innocent again . . .

And a few other
gormless ads followed
about lice,
mouth-ware,
full hair,
butterwhips,
cord shorts
and trolls . . .

Then there was a News Flash
about a woman
who'd just stabbed her granny
90 times
with a Phillips screwdriver,
and more backlash followed
about taxes
and betrayals
— then a quick smile
from the newsreader
for the *"good weather holding up"* —
and it was straight back
to the soap again,
like nothing
had even happened . . .

But that little detour
within a show,
within a show,
always shook Candy hard.
The way everyone
was just expected
to suddenly shuffle through

the tales,
and the bribes,
and the truths,
with undue regard
over what was ever
actually real
in the end . . .

She'd feel the guilt
suddenly wash over her,
just as her smile erupted;
when inherently,
she was still more than
aggrieved
over what she'd just witnessed
only seconds before . . .

And she wondered
if anyone else
— or maybe everyone else? —
was reeling under
the same charge as her,
trying to juggle it all
together . . .

"Society moving in for the kill?"
she'd think,
hearing the racket of the gangs
on the streets below.
Then Acquila was on screen,
at the news desk,
doing her worst:

". . . The Police Chief
had stated to the minister
in parliament
that his forces
could only ever detect
minor brainwaves
of malevolent intent
from protestors
with their portable
electrocephalographs."

Armoured lawmen
would cruise about the streets
on Segways,
like robot militia
of the 5th millennium,
armed with these gadgets
in their holsters,
coined *"De-willers"*
by those long persecuted
— strange gizmos
like opal lobsters.

TRIGGER ON THE WIND

Skimming the black belly
of a low hanging cloud,
a flying demon
devouring an apple
— with a ladder across his blades —
slowly glides down
to the tiny coastal town below,
spitting out pips
like they were the clitorises
of angels
across the mossed rocks
rusting in the shoals . . .

In their buttered-up lairs,
the town's weary merchants
softly resuscitate
their secret whims again,
snoring in the same old
dumb trance of lore . . .

With an egg's timid ear,
they listen to the inner heckling
still echoing
since long begun:
"Are you there?"
"Are you there?"

A dozen napping dogs,
in salty backyards,
suddenly sit up
from their mats
in unison,
as if summoned
by the blows
of so many hidden reeds . . .

Issue of an octave
from the underworld?
But from above;
settling upon them all
like the stray sonic waves
of a thousand
ravished bats . . .

Along Fizzing Bay,
the odd moonbeam
sieving through the cover
illuminates the crinkles of foam
peeling back from the shore
like some great withdrawing prepuce
about the circumference
of the world . . .

On old, rolled beds of cockleshells,
two cloven hooves *crack!*
like a thousand tiny traps
set for pestilence . . .

The shadow
of an emaciated devil
wavers across a dozen sandcastles
still standing sturdy
in medieval rows
along the strand . . .

In a seeming spell,
the somnambulists,
in their army,
each and all night-dressed,
and still in their socks,
are out in their forces,
quietly shuffling along
the sandy streets
in a daze,
unbeknownst
to each other . . .

The preoccupied dogs
still reeling
to the subtle shrill
ceaselessly harrowing them . . .

Hades' angel props his ladder
to the nearest pane,
and ascends,
rung by rung,
in deft burglar silence . . .

The window jimmied,
he enters the chamber
— fouling its very ambience —
as the town's sleepwalkers,
one by one,
in their slumbering gait,
topple in gradual accruement
from atop the high lime cliffs . . .

The first scout
of Satan's garrison
snuggles up asleep,
warm in a cobbler's
godly eiderdown;
awaiting the arrival of the dawn,
and his belated sentinels . . .

1993

(Image: Hieronymus Bosch)

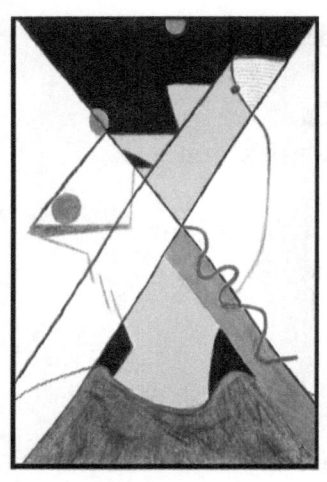

THE BIG BAD WORLD

"ATTENTION.
Agents of all stations.
This is the Director of the Bureau.
The old, fat, wigged, commie diva,
Jerzy Kesterov
— AKA Carson Lester,
"The Lounge Lizard" —
who publicly adorned himself
in expensive pelts,
who was a closet h-h-hammersexual,
long hooked on snow,
and privy to a constant supply
of moonshine,
and who had bulimia,
and was always puking up
gourmet food
in a porcelain bucket offstage,

just out of earshot
of all of his pinko fans
— all of whom he loathed
as "pinheads"
but suckled on like a lamprey! —
. . . ahem . . . is dead.
Pass it on.
To all informants.
PRONTO."

The way Edgar scrawls
the dated notion of *"sacrifice"*
on every hustled memo.
The way he coins
"defiling ancient devotions"
on the phones
to all his paranoid lackeys . . .

Little, dog-faced Edgar
grew up fatherless
in a backwater town,
dutifully raking mud
for his Uncle Fud, "The Inscrutable,"
where he soon developed
a distaste
for moral turpitude
in the company of his elders;
who all deemed him
an enigmatic paragon
of the first order,
like the whole world would . . .

"Alright now,
you freeze like a popsicle!"
was Edgar's first set-up arrest
for the papers,
surrounded by the cult of expertise
always in back of him
till his final breath . . .

The infamous gangster
snarled back
in the Chicago darkness,
"I am not an ice-box,"
then spun around
with pistols blazing,
 . . .fuckface!"

But after a long shoot-out
with his rookie agents,
the dust cleared,
and there was Edgar's deft spat
on the hood's bloody head
at the end,
and on the front page at last,
like the daffy elitism
of rich shooters on safari
in those days,
posing for all the encyclopaedists'
Kodaks . . .

F — W — O — O — S — H —

116

— [30 YEARS ON] —

"Jawline" Clyde,
seated at his little Tupperware desk,
in his see-through
secretary suit,
slowly typed:
CASE OF AN ARTIST
POSING AS CHRIST WITH A YOYO
— CLOSED.

"Done and dusted,"
he said aloud to himself,
filing it in the secret vault
for Edgar's private perusal.
But Edgar had gone home early
that day,
because he was still a little steamed
after spotting the graffiti
on the front of his building
when he'd first arrived
in the morning . . .

Overnight,
someone had added
in a neat copperplate scrawl
the glib remainder of three words
to the matching initials
of his powerful organization,
and now it said
FUCKING BIGOTS INC.

in gold capital letters out front
for all the public
to snicker at . . .

Clyde had whispered to him
to *"do something relaxing at home, Eddie,"*
like maybe finally trying on
his mama's wedding gown,
which was still wrapped up
in mothballs
with the last remains of her estate,
ever since her just recently
"un-grandmommied" life
had gone by way of the ether . . .

Anyway, Clyde vowed
to cheer Edgar up later,
that early summer eve.
He planned to drop around with roses,
spaghetti and chocolates,
and with a new LP
of Parisian accordion music
under his arm;
all poached clean
and puffed up in his talc
and cologne,
with his Flintstone jaw
cut smooth as a snake's,
and his teeth all glossy as a chimp's,
with his thick hair
slicked back in ostrich oil . . .

But later,
that sunny afternoon,
Edgar dourly surfaced
from his homestead
to walk his dozen tiny dogs
with his next-door neighbour,
the weather-beaten senator,
Bigfoot Lyndon . . .

Lyndon had these patchy old hounds
with sagging jowls,
and hides 10 sizes too big
for them,
and often,
as they'd scamper at lampposts
to relieve themselves,
Lyndon would brazenly
turn his back to the road
and water a neighbour's rosebushes
in broad daylight
—which always astounded Edgar,
who was always spick and span
and well-mannered,
in his pastel walking suit,
with his little fluffy pups,
who always looked like the wind
could just blow them
to smithereens,
like they were dandelions,
leaving nothing behind
but their bones . . .

Edgar and Lyndon
were long-time friends,
though Lyndon
was always left bewildered
by the many strange terms
Edgar often employed in conversation
— odd rat-a-tat words —
that he'd never heard before
over his many corrupt years
in the South,
like *"magna cum laude"*
and *"mimeograph"*
and *"cadre"*
and *"bivouac"*
and *"missive"*
and *"cudgel"*
and *"imbroglio"* this
and *"imbroglio"* that . . .

Whereas,
all Lyndon would yammer on about
was *"WINSOME, DITZY, BLONDE
GAMINS!"*
and *"SHOO-FLYS FROM OTHER
WORLDS!"*
and *"THE GREAT PEPPER TREES
OF TEXAS!"*
and *"ALL THE NEWSPAPER MORGUES!"*
and never about all those
coming in
or out of the cold . . .

120

At the end of their lap
around the block,
Lyndon stopped
at a neighbour's hydrangeas,
and — in broad daylight again —
let loose another stinking quart;
his huge belt-buckle
unfastened and dangling
in the Washington light,
as all of his ugly *"dowwwgs"*
did the same
to a trash can
in the gutter . . .

 "I may not know much, Ed . . . "
Lyndon seethed.

"You know plenty."

". . . but I know chicken shit
from chicken salad.
And I know this administration
is the worst thing
that's happened
to this country
since pantyhose ruined
finger-fuckin'!"

All their mismatched dogs
yapping away
at all the cars finning by,
as they huddled in a whisper,

aside the racket,
like two old shackled carnival barkers,
forever whipping up
something to flog
to all the Saturday-nighters . . .

~

Over time,
the country changed flavour
from blood to sky,
as the long cold years of the war
still inched along,
and many private nights passed by,
with Edgar and Clyde
still wrapped
in each other's federal arms,
for the fear
of their jobs . . .

But then,
that Thousandth Day cut down
— that gone black Texan noon —
letting loose
the great chthonic fear
across the earth,
and old Edgar's neck
was off the block again
as Lyndon took the reigns
of the Free World . . .

Old sly-boots Ed,
baiting his 7th stooge in a row
— *"Thirty-nine years!*
Top O' The World, Ma!" —
and still the world's
white bread icon
of virtue . . .

But he could finally sleep
peacefully again,
knowing he was tucked back deep
in the bosom
of his old benefactors once more;
all of them laughing it up
in the shadows
like kids at a magic show . . .

"All gone.
All gone.
All gone."

IN LIEU OF EMPIRE
(Timor-Leste, 1942)

A teenage platoon
of foreign soldiers
with broken eyes,
wielding machetes in their fists,
sorely slush through
the thick gravy marshes,
swinging at everything
in sight . . .

Splintered ivy
worms their filthy skins
as rhapsodic monkeys
water the nascent weeds.
And in the leaden air
— a stench of guano.

Five miles on:
shell-shocked hares
with elephantiasis
zigzag the daisy hills
as swooping ravens
fleet the meadows
from the hailing blitz . . .

Atop the ruins
of Coraceo Hill,
a lone pistachio tree

tinkles burnt nuts on a rock,
as bombed-deaf troops
in their final hours
— with their girls back home
forever fixed in their eyes —
spoon themselves together
like spent lovers
into a snug
reflecting
h u s k . . .

THAT GIRL CALLED "FOREVER"

Deep inside
The Royal Botanic Gardens
stands a colossal wall
built of peas
and toothpicks . . .

"Only a diamond
can cut a diamond,"
he says to her,
hanging flowers
around her swanny neck,
as she peers in
closely at it . . .

"Vomit of my past,"
she sighed.

"Sick patch of my future,"
he sighed back at her.

And she leant back
and laughed
in the spring rain,
suddenly dodging a kite
being pulled behind
a pony's tail . . .

Back on Spencer Street,
the paperboys wailed,
*"Thirty per cent
of all love birds
die of obesity!"*
as the couple waited
at the bus stop . . .

Everyone had fought over her
in the olden days
when she was tucked up
in the womb.
The donors of the seed
and the egg
had battled hard
with her surrogate mum
— and lost.
The courts were victorious.
The church defeated.
The media sated . . .

"Bye, Forever,"
he burbled,
staring into her eternity eyes.
Then he turned away
as the door slammed.
And he looked back
as the bus pulled out,
but she didn't wave
— or maybe
it was the filthy glass?

Then the racket resumed,
and he stepped back
into the throng,
and joined in,
barking stupid again . . .

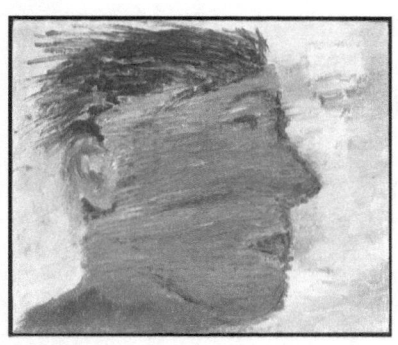

IN THE NIGHTFREE

As he sprawls out
in the old family hammock,
sucking down
the cold evening air
into his battered lungs,
the beacon's hazy glow
alights the bare
but foggy Cape . . .

His gentle eyes . . .
His damning mind . . .
His deathly memories . . .
His roaring thoughts . . .

He begins to gently wilt,
gently melt
into the years of dusty leaves
beneath him;
dreaming of his lost love,

and how he drank her
in every stolen breath
between shots . . .

Himself for himself again;
as had they all
before him,
in the one long family name . . .

No more apple in his neck
— dissolved in Guinness
and guzzled tears —
he took to the next world
imposed . . .

His deluded stab
at expressing his all . . .
Hastened attempts . . .
Hastened worth . . .

And his lack of love now,
and how he lay,
spluttering up
the soot of his lungs . . .

He'd long curtailed that trust
by venting
his own unsorry whims
when first
he'd let himself go . . .

Witless to her calls . . .
Heedless to her promises . . .
Mindless to her aches . . .
As he felt himself
as himself again . . .

He'd scrambled over
the broad expanse,
disloyally waving her away,
thinking of how
she must have thought
he'd obviously given up
on himself . . .

Before he'd briefly returned
to their original home,
she often wondered
of his paling skin,
and his then cold
deadening eyes.
He'd seemed not to care
for himself anymore . . .

Ever since he'd returned,
months before,
alone and unkempt,
he'd kept to himself,
having lost all;
and she knew
he still held dear
the notion
of his own demise . . .

He returning . . .
His one return . . .
Of he upon her . . .
And of his saving . . .

But now,
he couldn't even stomach
the notion
of returning that to her . . .

He'd clearly returned
more nervous of her,
but she didn't wish
to hurt him . . .

Her . . .
Her . . .
Hert him.

BY THE BIRTH OF MOONS

As orange convicts
in chains
across Iceland
scoop up stray puffins
from the snowed-in roads
— each bird blinded
by arctic light —
and box them up safely
overnight,
to free them offshore
at the crack of dawn . . .

. . . an opera crowd
in Sicily,
shaking the testicles of mules
in the air,
scream *"Long live the knife!"*
in unison
to the twee eunuchs
piercing Aida on stage.

And whilst
in foggy Peru,
as newly ordained nuns
scurry across the hills
at night,
yoking pails of lime juice
to the ailing wards
up high in the Andes . . .

. . . the ex-superintendent
of a zoo in Burkina Faso,
wheels his wife
in a wonky wheelbarrow
down a potholed road,
muttering under his breath
to the passing alien law
the mighty words
of Vinny V. Gone,
"Do not become
the slave of your model,"
and dumps his spouse
into the municipal pond
for her daily lather.

Then,
simultaneously,
in the middle of each ocean,
colossal
equilateral triangles
of undissolved solid blood
arise from the depths
like newborn isles,
and float away
like odd balloons
to the heavens,
to forever orbit the world
as moons,
casting the strangest
bloodshot haze
across the earth . . .

. . . all in lieu
of the many bloodied histories
long scribbled
by assassins.

GERT BY SEA

The billowing of the sea wind
hit *"young Gerty"* hard
in her wedding dress,
like a tornado
caught in a b/w photo . . .

Nearby,
an old boyfriend
called Dax
was staring at a rock
on the road
like he was thinking
of using it . . .

"In d'er own impermeable times,"
the Irish priest intoned
to the congregation,
"dey will still boat like each other
when quietly,
but indelibly, rising."

But such strong sympathies
never paddled space
more slowly,
more gruelly,
than from poor Dax
to Gert . . .

After six months
of going out together,
needing that old rich "he" again
— on the rebound —
she re-wrote
her old aromas
on the air,
and knowing Rory
to still speed-walk
his old suburban nightmare
as usual,
she took to the Tan as well,
and his eyes again,
and not Dax's anymore . . .

Gert sprawled herself out
across Rory's couch
like the golden days,
buttering up
her greening heart again,
and threw out
another reminiscent laugh to him;
and she knew immediately
on hearing his *"gurgle"*
from the kitchen
he was snared again . . .

So she puffed herself up
like a dove
and let loose another
more subtle purr

— but in a less existential tone
than before —
and he came scuffling out
as expected,
like a loyal dachshund
expecting a bone . . .

"Soul-mates,"
she softly said to him
as they finally kissed,
"like we said."

The moonlight
soon shimmering off
their sweating skins
like they were mirrors
themselves . . .

"They seemed veritably prosperous."
— a tourist's glib laughter
broke close behind Dax's ears,
and was suddenly gone
on the sea wind
beyond him . . .

He stamped out his cheroot
and took to the steps again,
and rushed back inside the church,
just in time to see them
seal the deal . . .

(Whilst in back of everyone,
the local winos had snuck in
and were quietly devouring
what was baked
like famished boars.)

But as the final sermon
unfolded,
an old nun dropped to the floor,
and trembled uncontrollably
in rapture,
frothing up the pulp
of a million
transubstantiated wafers,
as the first Irish ear-bashing
began to toll . . .

 "Because of dis,"
the priest said
— holding his arms out wide
like he was crucified —
*"some say Jesus died
at quarter to t'ree.
But everyone knows
He died at t'ree o'clock,
as Mat'hew noted,
Chapter 27, Voice 45.
But dat doesn't mean
He died like dis, does it?"*
And he quickly moved one arm
to high noon . . .

"You can't see His face!
The crux was not a clock, people!
Our Saviour was not a sundial!
What is da time to do . . ."

And an old sea dog yelled out
from the back
— looking at his bare wrist —
"Quarter after nine,
to be sure, Farda,"
before fleeing
with the cake
and his hearties . . .

NUKED CITY

In burnt rags
they swam this homely bay,
this hot and sticky city brine,
with all the dead dolphins
floating by
in melted swarms . . .

and they all cupped
their way through
the heaving crests,
with the moon
de-sickled to a spear;
a colossal needle
as sharp as a broken smile
at every end . . .

and there were
the high hungry fires
for miles,
spaghetti-ing along the shores,
with the milky sand
all spat up and hocked
like a boiling
bubbling nougat
everywhere . . .

and they all waddled along
a shallow bank,
with their feet burning

on the slippery bed
— the whole sky burnt white
with corpse —
and the tussled hairs
of the scape inside
still sizzling
like overdone dogs . . .

but there was always the dream
of a certain offer
that kept them all on,
as they dragged
their battered ears
for a simple crick
to the beyond,
with a simple faith
in the clay,
that would
— one inglorious day —
more humbly swallow them . . .

THE HIERARCHY OF BROKEN AIMS

Patriots with their dreams,
rebels with their ideals,
martyrs with their fevers,
all in the same long, motley breath,
clambering home
like lemmings
to the edge . . .

Down in old *"Bearbrass"*,
the mills grind their mash
as the showground llamas
stare up bored at the sky
gently spitting on the road . . .

And like junkies on stilts,
an endless stretch
of twisted ghost gums
by the kerb
gasp for gulps
of the peak-hour smog . . .

People with no profiles
storm along
in their huddles,
in silent queues and gangs,
catching cabs
and buses
and trains,
all with dog meat

in their knaps,
and kitty litter
under their arms,
and show bags
in their hands,
with maybe chocolates
and toys inside . . .

All of them silently gassing
in their packs,
as they interweave
within the hail . . .

And the only
cheered one around?
The ex-con in his donut-van,
selling a hundred holes an hour;
gleaning with every sugar hound
he was once a *"wholesaler"*
from the start:
"Get it?"
he repeats to everyone,
"D'ja get it?"

The voids
that are cudded by all
as they dourly splatter puddles
all the way home! . . .

And the racket
in their ears
as they sulk
about the day's morass. . .

All returning back home,
in their stately sufferance,
to the safety
of their lazy dogs
and lives;
and smeared across their eyes
like a permafrost,
the dear ancient appeal
of their wasted youth
— their dreams
and ideals —
in hock.

MANY DIFFERENT
INSTANT HISTORIES

A poor infant girl
swathed in cloth,
with cauliflower ears
and golden bangs,
had many different fathers,
from many different worlds . . .

The 1st was a Ditch Witch digger.
The 2nd, a driver for dog trailer tippers.
3rd, a cruciverbalist.
4th, a retiring thaumaturgist.
And the last was a
photovoltaic researcher . . .

Each 11th hour
in her hometown, Laarp,
the local police
pull their hair out
as they sift through
all the abandoned
matryoshka dolls . . .

Gone are all the old,
misdemeanoured days
of odd thefts of anoraks
from Wool Board Road,
and all the ragged miscreants
spraying snide phrases

across the factory walls,
like *UNICEF RHYMES
WITH DEATH* . . .

All the locals are knee-deep
in the manufacture
of home-made mortar bombs now.
The police find gangs
huddling about
the derelict boatsheds,
whipping up their
hick glycerine kits
to plant outside
the town hall . . .

The law has seen
the slaughter
of so many affluent souls
in their new apartments
along the quay . . .

They've heard
all their whelps
in the night . . .

They've scooped up
their prized bluing brains
from the gutters
like hocked-up jellyfish
along the shitty shores
of the bay . . .

And they've heard
all the night growls by the drome;
only to find each trotter
daubed with fangs . . .

The poor infant girl
swathed in cloth,
with cauliflower ears
and golden bangs,
who had many indifferent fathers,
from many indifferent worlds,
is dead . . .

Her ma is out
in the search for love
to start all over again . . .

She blindly rushes off
to the richest clan nearby
— partying hard —
learning no lessons
from the many
post-coital semblances
of angels about,
sympathetically caressing her hair,
thinking each
unpummelled stroke in the dark
was but the secret,
gentle touchings
of the men . . .

INTO THE VIOLENT SILENCE

Empty rivers
ghostly crawl
as bats float by
like hats in a storm . . .

Conical farmers
round sheep
to squared-off ponds
like shrinks
with all their
wooden blocks . . .

That's all you can see.

Where is the worm
when everything is done?

*"This is a laughing hill
we're on,"*
Denny gasped
to a stranger
making the climb as well,
*"there's a monster
underground."*

On top of Uluru,
the wind blew a label
onto Denny's shoe;

it was made
on the other side
of the world . . .

. . . g a a a a h h h h . . .

In the blistering heat,
a molting crow
regurgitates the sooty talc
of its sheen . . .

Flashing marbles
fall from the sky
as lightning retches
a dry-reaching spark . . .

And fleas
fly through the air
the size of dogs . . .

What is fire
and dormant crackles of ash?

. . . g a a a a h h h h h h h h . . .

Copters curdle by
as the dragonflies
buzz low
from the spinifex shoots . . .

In the red dust,
footprints turn into potholes;
there's no one inside to grow.
Everyone's driving their dreams
back home . . .

"Snatch a cloud,
you laughing birds.
The world's spinning
like a top."

Lumps of sleep
in Denny's eyes
crumble away like clay,
as the fat bugs buzz by,
blue winged,
orange sacked,
ROARING
into the red hot stillness
of the day . . .

Uluru, 1987

IMPLOSIONS AND EGGS

Carl renders all forces
of the plundered game,
back, back, and *back*,
to the simple ill purr
of her name
and easy grandeur.

Or was that shame?

In her doomed
but comely eyes,
long blazed the spoors
of shooting stars;
and whilst everyone's blood
ran lean with want,
she took solace
in the glean
of all that once riven again.

Or was that torn?

In lieu of all her mastered ploys,
the laboured designs
of all her airy pet schemes
have plummeted to the earth
like great slices of tripe
fallen peeled
from the nails
of the most filthiest gods!

Or were they
just the remnants
of yet another fleeing atom
in shreds?

Carl has misread all that
so misseen,
as has her chiselled features
butchered all
who ever sought
to claim a simple plane;
and for like,
as the birds fly by him again,
in flames,
he offers up his pump,
once more,
so privately primed,
to explode in her mitts.

Or was that in exchange?

IN TOMATO TOWN

With leftover snook
in their arms,
and under their pits,
and in their rusted buckets,
the tourists lashed out large
on the local mongers
for such a fresh haul of bait
to hook more yellowtail
by day's end . . .

Spied through a crack
in the fence,
the keeper stacked his abalone
back in the crates,
then returned to the hatch;
but the poachers
were already strangling
the guard dog in back,
planning which dock
they'd raid first
for the simplest of caches . . .

To the sketch artist
the monger reported:
"One face with hard, focused eyes.
With the other one
that was balding,
but wiry."

Such fully bared heads
were not all that common then,
assured the sergeant . . .

Over the squad car radio,
a giggly KALOF bulletin
was soon issued,
all senseless,
with elan,
and slurred esses:
"Similar features,
that endear rapport
with others,
the world over,
unconsciously congregate
in broken mirrors."

Everyone in town
— even the law —
were bent on something . . .

"Get off the radio, Lonni."

"Pass it on," she snickered,
as she clearly took
another toke;
the airwaves burbling . . .

THE BUTCHER'S PERCH

A shut eye
embossed in each leaf
is how little Mackie
sees a snapshot of G-d
at His first glance . . .

The dead tree
like a shadow of His hand
clutching at Himself
as He flees the world
for the last time . . .

Beneath —
His old skin lies in ruins.
The rocks:
the shedded rags of His youth.
And over there,
the waterfall,
His first infantile thought;
the sound of eternity
harking back
to His first day at play . . .

The birds flit by
across His brow.
A lagoon at each corner
of His mouth.
A red gum
above His nose . . .

156

Early enough,
we'll forgo His first toy
for the beyond
as well,
where more worlds are waived,
awaiting
the next butcher's perch . . .

LAUGHTER'S DOLL

Two old eyes
stuck firmly
on a bygone crime,
beyond a tilted glass;
each one reared in law,
but not in lieu
of themselves
anymore . . .

He's lifted up the book of life
with old ham-fists
for an eternity,
all just for the sake
of forging some flagrant bond
with the next world . . .

He's seen them all
prancing about
each Sunday dawn,
in mock-heroics;
at first gallant,
then histrionic,
with the same old tired pride;
all cruelled
like misfired seers,
and for what
in the end
— a basic mud?

Is he mad, too?
he often wonders,
bereft of calmatives;
a log stuffed cold
with censured fears,
immovable with ache,
a certain lag;
and inside,
a muddied heart
without the stomach to march.

Unlike how
they all see themselves,
without bordered oaths anymore;
irrefutable,
and with busted guns . . .

Yet, all he fears
between his ears,
is the sour cachinnations
of laughter's doll . . .

TOES TO THE GRINDER

All the world's leaders
are calling corpses
"fools" now;
just like the old slurs
Caligula coined in his day,
before anointing his horse
a priest . . .

"It'sa gooda for the newa generations,"
they all rib each other
at the U.N.,
as they guzzle down
their rat lagers
in disrepair;
slumming within
the new boundaries
of decency and disgrace . . .

The old sky soon spun
its battered bag about,
and up till dawn,
each star gleaned
its beloved beauty again;
though for a time,
only the moon
could be seen above the province,
stuck like a spotlight
over everyone . . .

But the muckraker
only had eyes for Flotsam.
He'd loyally observed
her grace and subtleties
from afar
for millennia . . .

His shifting, tolling span
had known no other.
Once, when she was sleeping,
he sneakily dipped his toes
inside her hands for solace;
but she had paws
like the great jaws of jewfish,
and left him hobbling
for all eternity . . .

Century after century,
he'd limped after her
so devotedly;
little caring of his failing gait,
and the heights still left
to clamour after her . . .

She'd crippled many
in her quest
to find her own
unknown beloved;
still on the loose somewhere,
unfounded,
and ever less obvious . . .

Flotsam had brilliant, boiling, olive eyes,
a wide, sultry mouth,
and the wiry white hair
of some afeard god
from mythology . . .

She'd long taken
each measure in her stride
with fortitude;
and he, the muckraker,
like a lame dog
— nonplussed —
had long continued
to trail her . . .

There was no effort
by either of them
to ever surrender their hearts
to any of those
they each seduced
on their every odyssey;
paying no heed to those
ever seeking
the same sort of
soulful replenishment . . .

They'd each soon met enough
of the damned,
and furthered each
to their own passion,
to attract only those smitten
by the same sensibility . . .

162

But for each
their unsated desires,
they would both
ceremoniously fillet time;
sieving the very seconds
for a mere clue
to the other's
long lost whereabouts . . .

The muckraker had dared
to put his toes to the grinder,
and Flotsam,
her sullen will to the call
forever distilling them;
both limping
in their own fashion,
in the dream
to at last hold one another
— but never
in the ghoulish skin
of each sharing alien.

SEWER SIDE

The music fest
faintly echoed
beyond the farmed hills,
as a packed van
rolled to a stop
on the shoulder of the highway;
trying to start again . . .

"Is that The Church, Ella?"
asked Golga
— meaning the band —
as she got out,
listening to one side . . .

"Ja," Ella said,
as she lumbered off
down the road
with her husband
and his guitars . . .

"Is the car low?"
Golga asked again,
with a frown,
too hungover to walk on . . .

"Ja," someone else
in the group said,
passing the bass drum
to someone else,

revealing the band's new English name
in dripping black:
"SEWER SIDE".

"We have no juice left."

And the others
went on ahead as well . . .

"Are . . . lies . . . gone . . .
young chap?"
Golga's 3rd crack at English,
to the shy young man
wearing Ray-Ban's
by the open window
in the back seat . . .

But he said nothing,
and just sat there.

"Man of hell . . ."
she slurred,
as she leaned in close to him
with a smile,
"take a nip of my gin
and grey ink,"
offering up
her secret silver flask
to his lips . . .

But he just stared ahead.
Then the drummer intervened
to tell her,
that the hitchhiker
was actually dead . . .

1991

CRANK DUDGEON

Old Parka was sent
a proviso parcel
from the outside:
soft paper rolls
of sweet lavender
for the rectum.

(Each ply secretly laced
with a pulp hallucinogen
that dissolves on the palate.)

But they were soon pinched
by old Jag in 32,
and he wound up
with a bleeding hole
and a mind gone awry.

He's diarrhetic now.
Colon fell to a brain
gone tawdry.
Lost half his weight in 2 days
and most of his concepts.

He just sits there in his cell now,
gurgling like a dog
junked on dynamite;
ever less homely
for its wrangles.

FANTE ON HIGH

In the flash cruiser jet,
old Fante mulls over
the tabloid cartoon
still echoing across his mind
since dawn
as he flinches to the throes
of the craft
swiftly charioting him . . .

It's blue inside,
but outside it's night,
and the light
from the locker above him
is exactly the same size
as the moon . . .

He secretly holds a finger
against the pinprick
inside his elbow;
then his eyes felt clearer . . .

All the end-of-the-week commuters
were empty in their faces;
their eyes glazed over
every rounded port of glass . . .

The hostess was sitting down,
green in dress,
and demeanour,

and then she softly hummed
a song to herself,
and no one moved,
as if they were all
suddenly dead on impact . . .

The senator
had boarded the plane
as he did every Thursday night
at the end of each sitting fortnight
in parliament.
He had his plastic bag
full of meat as usual,
though this time
it was the head of a hog.
He flashed it to the hostess,
and she shyly twiddled
with its long hairy ears
as she pulled a face,
and then it was all wrapped up again,
and they just sat there,
near each other,
saying nothing as usual
for the third season in a row . . .

The jet made a soothing purr
that bound everyone together.
It meant no one had to cough,
or feel nervous
about anything
for a while . . .

A head or two
only turned once in a while
when a white cloud whizzed by
on the other side,
and then the tranquillity was back
just as quickly again . . .

Hours later,
back down to Earth
on an interstate tarmac,
the pilot had missed the line,
and had to get down
to realign the wheel,
but still no one moved inside;
just their homesick eyes
forever glued to the glass
like they were televisons . . .

They could each only
still see themselves though,
dreaming of the magnetism of snow,
as it began to softly fall outside,
all about them,
smothering everything . . .

AS PHOEBE SOFTLY PERCHES

Phoebe's crimson nose
is like the delicate beak
of a Java sparrow,
and her skinny limbs
are all finely feathered too
— if caught in the right light —
but she never flies . . .

She wears a lurex,
pinstriped walking outfit
everywhere she goes,
like she carries around with her
a pet bird's grievous quarters.
The bars are all over her.
And all the grocers
always run their scanners
across her, too,
like the tubs of yogurt in her fists,
just to make sure
she's really there,
because she's so pale
and thin . . .

But she's got
this strangely naive nature,
which — although too,
is like a tamed bird's —
seems to disguise a certain
overwhelming fatalism

she tries not to
ever openly exude,
and from which she can't ever
fully absolve herself from
— because of her beauty —
and take flight from . . .

She sings sweetly too
— away from anyone
who knows her —
with her strange piccolo tongue,
and the rapid warble
in her throat
when she's happy . . .

But crewcutted Phoebe
knows now
— as do all her cronies in back —
that she will never
fully free herself,
from her self,
unless the many men
purring *"Foodies"* in her ear
cease tossing her
all their paltry crumbs . . .

But she's
"got survival down pat now,"
she tells anybody
who cares to hear . . .

She doesn't need
no more help.
Because she's got
"the falling acorns everywhere"
to grow her own trees
if need be,
and all those
"early worms
popping up everywhere
like the periscopes of fate"
to guide her
the safest way on . . .

A 2 B

One whipped-up scheme
of revenge,
with heft
— all steely-mapped,
but mild to the touch —
suddenly smacks hard
into the dearest dream,
like a tug
gutting up
against a berg . . .

And the rank pong of thought
— a stupid fog,
mustered as a snotted pearl,
a newborn lie,
a sticking hurt —
lays back,
unjust,
for the whim
without . . .

And out for the same glean
for all,
wave all the long gone
murdered vows
and promises
again . . .

And now,
a dead bird lands
at every door at dusk,
and for the zillionth time,
the same old buttered
sunrise . . .

Like a bullet,
re·aimed in focus,
go all these same done
daily reminders
of the end
to come . . .

THE DECLARATION TODAY IS DISINVENTION

Out of his bare back,
it hangs,
he's sure . . .

He thinks
it's like a newborn calf
with an inflamed hooter
or something . . .

Miles aims his eyes
like dreams
into the glass,
to see behind
what all along
drags him down
when others are watching . . .

Fore and aft, fore and aft,
looking around,
with another's look
in regard . . .

Outside in the gloom,
sits the rusted heap,
still stinking burnt from tries,
as the purple clouds of Melbourne
gurgle by,
grinding monkey sounds . . .

He's shut the gates
and opened them,
and still doesn't know
what to watch for.
He makes plans
to abscond at times,
and then the old blade cuts in
to short-circuit any hope
for luck again . . .

In his mind,
heaven is just the hum
of the road beyond,
with nothing
but the tight flesh of his face
to twist around;
no longer blind to the surprises
of each stuttered symptom
of his soured life
in consequence . . .

His feet are wet
and clogged with earth,
and his eyes are open like dahlias
to receive the charge again;
but still,
nothing quite garnishes a heart
near culled
like a churning sea outside,
swilling down
every dream
in abeyance . . .

Miles wishes the world
a dozen special things;
but no wish comes true,
but lies . . .

Now he's resigned
to a less loftier mirage,
like all those living
more interior lives;
forever gambling
with each nurtured
inhibition . . .

THE ECHO INDUSTRY

Amongst the ruins
of a colosseum
teeming with zephyrs,
laughing tourists
on the ancient stage
honk out loudly like seals
to the back rows
as they sliver down mussels
with shots of ouzo . . .

Nearby,
hooded gulls
weave across the azure shore
like moths
warmed to light bulbs,
skimming the broken edges,
where kids and dogs
splash about
like dying tuna . . .

CIRCLES OF MUD

One of the world's worst lies
is that there's no fire
beyond the eyes
when dissolved in reverie;
that the mind
simply atrophies
like a pastry roll
abandoned
to the gloaming . . .

Why was one eye,
one ear,
not enough
to absorb the chaos?

Why was that lone wet crack
in the jaw,
to just sprawl there,
like a murdered dog
on a spring lawn
just freshly watered?

Tully wants to cut off an ear
like Vince
and trust his first impression.
He wants to pluck out an eye
like Cyclops
and press for instinct.

He wants less alternatives,
and more mouths
to bark out his begorrahs!

But now,
those old bones
are just dragged along,
like a gambler
with a sack of cans
to cash in
for pittances . . .

His heart
is simply a pump
to siphon out the gruel
flooding the lower ballasts
of a lost rite of passage . . .

The world's best lie
is that there's a fire
before the eyes
when immersed
in censure . . .

TEARS AS A CHAIR

A giant, open clam
with a big blue eye
slowly blinks
on the subterranean floor . . .

In its reef-wracked skull,
it looks around,
parting wistful glances
at the long deadly whips
of a bluebottle
trailing by . . .

To the side;
a sly starfish
slowly crawls by
like a fly . . .

And this eye,
this lonely spy,
cries *oceans* . . .

BREATH OFF A SPIDER'S LIPS

Tomb to tomb tsetse flies.
Horror stars buzzing by,
dripping devil's blood . . .

"The Apostles
were Christ's press,"
the vicar spieled
at the gravesite.
"One had an adding machine.
Another, a sextant."

Afar, a bad statue
of an infamous liar
— with no hope
of ever entering
the submarine world —
dissolved Aspro-clear in the haze
fizzing above
the crematorium . . .

"Go fuck a shoe!"
laughed all the mourners at the end,
dancing away free
and suddenly unfeeling again . . .

Fucking hell.
Our flimsy webbed suicides.

1990

TIME

Whilst swallowing up
everything,
like history,
television,
worms,
and sharks,
measurable
or immeasurable,
with its old murderous hands
— all hiccupped
and hullaballooed —
each daunted sperm
scrambles in ubiquitous need
to embrace the source . . .

When all along,
known
or unknown
— and never grasped —
time lays each cell back down,
one by one
to the clay
— both hands
stretching the great maw
at the end,
as begun —
gorging each sallow day,
the mistook to the raid
in their tattered costumes . . .

CONCOURSE OF THE SPIRITS

At times,
like art on exhibition,
reality unsubtly shears its scabs,
revealing the three states
that scare you most;
love, pain, and existence.

Meanwhile,
on the roof,
your father lands as a sparrow
at the end
like in a postcard
from the beyond . . .

Now
— and this is for everyone —
even the mad buggers
falling poor as mice
in the storms . . .

*"We were all made yesterday,
and that was once
immediately."*

LISTEN.

*"A long time ago,
before the first smile erupted,
before time was pleased*

to duly suffocate us all,
you were quiet
somewhere . . .
waiting your turn."

THE WASTING WEEDS

The weathervane spins.
The church is full.
The coffin
— with a beanie and skis
crossed on top —
is dragged past pews,
ice pick by ice pick . . .

The tub out front idles on.
Uncles and friends,
and bunnies-in-beanies
carry the casket out . . .

Everything *stings* . . .

The varnish drips
on this sunny day.
Later, mourners find the soles
of their feet
sticking to the footpath.
They curse out loud
as they scrape them on the gutter,
and storm off
like show-horses
down the street,
lifting their knees
higher and higher . . .

"His face was stitched up,"
everyone said.

*"The back of his head
was stuffed like a pillow."*

*"He looked peaceful.
Except for that smirk."*

The needle.
The thread.

Slow cars
lit like ovens
blundered by . . .

The dirt fell heavy
like concrete
into the hole;
a beaten bass drum . . .

Everywhere,
the ground green and soggy . . .

The musical beats
of shattering tears
on the weeds,
the beautiful weeds . . .

1986

O FOR 10 YEARS OF CRUMBS

Once,
when he was young,
and out *"scunging"* on the range
for a lark,
because of a sudden gossip
spun
about the grind at work,
he soon washed his remarks
of the locals
and promptly quit his job
at the family station,
then sat back,
resuming his ideals,
feeling somewhat sure
of everything . . .

Then the wet,
vessel-squirting carcass
of the gardener
smashed through the window,
landing beside him
in his sleep,
with a cut noose
around its neck;
squelching,
farting,
dying . . .

Hours later
in the silence,
the cook and the farrier
helped him wrap it up
in their hammocks,
and they buried it
out the back
near the lemon tree grove
where their grandpas
used to piss . . .

1985

THE EGGS OF LULL

Over time,
the language in her eyes
subtly fades
by the blinks . . .

and exits
in the tears
streaming down
her swollen cheeks . . .

till they bury
into the rash of her nostrils,
and burrow down
into the *"wound"*
of her mouth . . .

"The irony of it all,"
she thinks,
"filling up my trap."

She swallows the tears down
in gulps,
till her gut percolates
with their congesting memories;
and the blood
whirls them all round,
sucking the protein out
— untainted.

Later,
at her usual monthly dip
at the baths,
she humbly pisses them all out
into the ocean . . .

Meanwhile,
their dampening effect
weighs her down
like an anchor;
like a bloodied anchor
of ghosts . . .

THE CIRCUS

Outside,
amongst the racket,
old bloated comics
pawn off their coded jokes,
as a litany of trumpets
wrangle
a dozen tonsils
in the distance . . .

To one side,
15 dwarves
dare drums with wooden eels,
whilst The Bearded Lady
blows a Eucharist-flute;
and a generic herd
slips into The Big Top
to see the matinee show . . .

A dipso-conjurer
teleports rabbits for luck,
as viscous rain
sags into a hanging toffee
from the tent ropes
— like stilts of vanilla stew —
and as bread on pianos
rust shag green
into prodigal metal . . .

A conga line
of prancing peafowls
strut their plumage
about the ring,
like conquistadors
on their passage home,
laden with spoils . . .

Aside,
a trail of ants
spy on a fist of bees
mobbing roses
with bitter threats . . .

THE RIVER IS A MIRROR

♫ *Valder-eeee* . . .
Valder-ahhh . . .
Valder-eeee . . .
Valder-ah-ha-ha-ha . . . ♫

The man
who sweetly sang a song
into a hollow log
by the Yarra's edge
suddenly quietened . . .

A woman gunned him down.

His little boy
quickly paddled away
in his father's canoe . . .

Nearby, a water rat
stopped building its home
in the shallows,
as the woman
slipped the dead man
inside the log,
on which
he'd only just sat
to sing echoes into
for his son . . .

Later,
on Herring Island,
another dad appeared
with a fishing rod
and his only son.
And the woman
gunned him down too.
And with the help of his boy,
they squeezed him
into the log as well . . .

The woman
gave the boy
her flimsy raft,
and he paddled away,
as the rat continued
to build its home,
undeterred . . .

She then shot herself
in the head,
and the bloodied lead
spewed from her skull,
dropping her remains
onto the rat's
home-sweet-home,
slowly sinking it
like a submarine
in a dive . . .

So the rat
slipped into the log
to live,
and the four open eyes
of the dead fathers
reflected the sun
and the moon,
day and night,
till summer 's end . . .

1984

THAT KILLING CLEM

"Amuse me, now,"
said young Christian Bob.

"Later, Robert,"
slurred his decadent dad,
firing up the sunlamp.

"But I need a laugh right now!"

"Later, I said!"

Bob stood waiting,
drinking his Milo.
Dad's name was Clem
and he downed
all his *"pixie"* pills . . .

The clock ticked
against its glass
on the kitchen wall
as his kids did the dishes . . .

And they stacked them high
in the cupboards;
but a tea-towel was tossed
— suffocating the time —
and all the lights
in the kitchen went out . . .

Clem suddenly crashed
to the floor as a clump
in the twilight,
and his jaws sprung open,
scuttling a horseshoe·row
of top teeth
across the lino
like a puck on ice . . .

Everyone at the table
lifted their hockey·stick feet
in the air
to let it pass out the back door.
(Someone whispered *"Goal!"*)

Then,
with their battered ma,
the four of them
clutched his carcass,
and dragged it upstairs,
and lugged it down
the dim hallway,
and flung it
onto the high bed,
reeking with a musky quilt . . .

And across the road,
through the open window,
fell the jarring din
of an old piano
and many heaving ballerinas . . .

THE TOWN CRIER

"Hold that fire!"
cried the town crier.

The four detainees fainted
as the squad
lowered their rifles.

"Go home, you bastards,"
whispered the sour General.
"We've got the wrong people,"
they heard him say.

The men were apologised to,
and they got up and left.
And they left a pool of sweat,
and not blood as expected.

The General went home.
And the town crier
sat in the town square
and waited to be needed again.

The General slumped in the pagoda
to savour his cocktail.
But his wife came out
and asked him
where their son was.
The General's mouth said,
"I don't know."

The General knew.
And so did the town crier.
Together, they were the same.
Apart, they were different.
He burned his certificate.
He burned the certificate of his birth.

That night,
his wife cried
as the General made love to her.

The next day,
the mother cried
the day her son died.

The troops were responsible.
The General wore sunglasses.
There was no opposition.
There was no town crier.

EVERYTHING DRAGS
ALONG LIKE HONEY

Do you feel as though
you have no internal shield,
and that at any second,
without any injury
of a physical nature,
your blood
will suddenly flow
out of the pores
of your skin,
just as easily
as it flows
within?

GIVEN EMBERS ALL

Hats on peoples' heads
blow off in the wind.
Gloves on purple hands
grip tight beneath teeming snow . . .

Tongues hide
in the back of dry mouths.
Eyes blink as much
as the lost birds
flap to the trees . . .

The chimney is covered.
The windows bolted.
The door locked.
The logs slowly burn . . .

Teased skin
gradually exposes itself
to the flames.
Finally a smile opens up
in the room . . .

The floorboards creak.
Two shoes clomp.
A fragrance in the air.
The woman naked . . .

She kisses the distant fire
as it crackles . . .

He wonders how a dream
can be drawn
without the need for it . . .

She touches him.

They move . . .

They make love . . .

1983